PURSUIT OF THE

PURSUIT OF THE

VIPER

Mike Bell

Beacon Hill Press of Kansas City
Kansas City, Missouri

Printed in the
United States of America

ISBN 083-411-6863

Editor: Bruce Nuffer
Assistant Editor: Kathleen M. Johnson
Cover Design: Mike Walsh
Cover Illustration: Keith Alexander
Inside Illustrations: Ron Garnett

Note: This book is part of the *Understanding Christian Mission,* Children's Mission Education curriculum. It is designed for use in Year 3, Compassionate Ministries. This study year examines the importance of helping others. Love-Link Ministries is an actual compassionate ministries center located in Oklahoma City.

10   9   8   7   6   5   4   3   2   1

Contents

Contents

CHAPTER 1

The Breath of Fear

Lenny's heart raced wildly as he climbed the last flight of stairs to a rundown apartment on the fourth floor. The climb did not make his heart race. Four flights of stairs were nothing to Lenny. His heart raced because he was afraid.

Leaning against the wall in the Dallas apartment building, Lenny tried to steady himself before knocking on door number 43. As he took a deep breath, he noticed how bad the old building smelled.

Staring at the door, its number written in black Magic Marker, he raised his hand to give the special knock.

Knock, wait two counts; knock, knock, knock, wait two counts; knock.

He heard steps from behind the door, then the sound of locks turning. Suddenly the door flung open, and Lenny stood looking into the bloodshot eyes of Viper Grimes.

"Get in here. You're late," Viper hissed.

Lenny stepped in quickly as the gruff figure closed and bolted the door.

Viper gave a twisted smile. Lenny cringed when he saw Viper's dingy yellow teeth. A bare bulb hanging from the ceiling reflected a dim light on Viper's shaved head. He towered over Lenny.

"Did you bring it?" Viper asked.

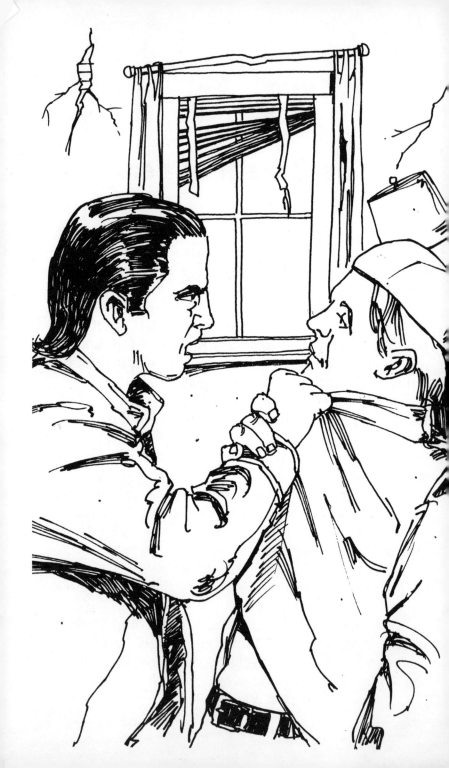

"Th . . . th . . . there was a l-l-l-i-i-i-ittle problem," Lenny hesitated.

Viper clenched his fists. "What kind of problem?" he growled, taking a step toward Lenny.

"W . . . w . . . w . . . wait, Viper, I can explain!" Lenny fell backward onto an old wooden chair. "I put the money in the backpack just as you told me. On my way here I kept checking behind me to make sure I was alone. That's when I saw Romero's guys."

"Romero!" Viper's eyes blazed with anger as he spoke the name.

"Viper, I was too far from here to start running. They would have caught me for sure," Lenny whimpered.

"Where's the money?" Viper screamed, jerking Lenny to his feet.

Lenny explained what happened to the pack full of money. Viper's face grew red. Lenny shut his eyes. When he opened them, Viper's red face was only an inch away.

"Listen very carefully," Viper growled. "You've got until 6:00 tonight to find my money. Otherwise, Weasel, your permanent home will be a hole in the ground. Now get out of here."

Viper unlocked the door and flung Lenny into the hallway. Lenny jumped up and stumbled down the stairs. He knew Viper didn't make threats; he predicted the future.

* * *

"Mommy, are you mad at us?" five-year-old Emy asked, looking up at her mother. Blake, her older brother, sat next to her in the front seat of the old station wagon.

Mary Redman's knuckles were white from gripping the steering wheel so tightly. She was mad, but not at her children. For the last four months, she worked nights at a food warehouse. But the company laid her off. Finding and keeping a job had been hard for Mary over the last five years. Now, after losing this job, she was ready to give up. After collecting her final paycheck of $60, she had come back to their rundown apartment. She gathered the children and their few belongings and headed out of town.

"No, Emy, I'm not mad at you," Mary answered, patting her daughter on the knee. "I'm just mad at life."

Mary's husband had left just before Emy was born. Life had been rough since then. Most of the work Mary found was only temporary, and she barely made enough money to put food on the table. The only apartments Mary could afford to rent were usually rundown and falling apart.

"Maybe we could visit Grandma," Blake said, staring out the side window.

Mary glanced over at her son. Blake didn't say much. When he did, he always sounded older and wiser than his 10 years.

Grandma, Mary's mother, lived in Wichita, Kansas. Five years earlier she and Mary had an argument, and Mary had not spoken to her since. She had wanted to many times. Mary had no money for a phone. She didn't know what to write. It was easier to just do nothing.

"Well, God," Mary prayed silently, "I know You must hate me. If You will help us get to Wichita, I'll at least know You don't hate my children." She quickly brushed a tear away before it could roll down her cheek. Then she headed the old car north on Interstate 35 toward Oklahoma and beyond to Kansas.

CHAPTER 2

Walk the Talk

"All right, will everyone please find a seat." Twenty youngsters in Mrs. Magill's fourth and fifth grade Sunday School class began to settle into their chairs.

"Kate, doughnuts are not Frisbees. Please wipe the chocolate icing off the wall," Mrs. Magill instructed. "Louie, I think the pencils would work better if you took them out of your nose."

After some announcements and a prayer, Mrs. Magill began the lesson.

"Last week we talked about the fruit of repentance," Mrs. Magill began. "Does anyone remember what that means?"

As usual, Sonia Tate quickly waved her hand in the air. Mrs. Magill could have asked how many miles to the moon, and Sonia would have raised her hand. Her answers were usually wrong, but she loved to talk.

"Yes, Sonia, tell us what we learned about this kind of fruit."

"It's an apple," Sonia said.

Several people giggled, including Sonia, as she continued with her answer.

"My dad told me that in the Garden of Eden, Eve baked an apple pie. God became angry because it was not cherry or peach. Then Adam ate some and got in trouble too. He resented apples from that day on. That's why they're the fruit of resentment."

Most of the class doubled over in laughter. Sonia wasn't sure why, but she laughed right with them.

"Thank you, Sonia," Mrs. Magill said. "I'd like to talk with you later about the Garden of Eden. Now, I'm asking about the fruit of repentance, not resentment."

"Oh, sorry," Sonia giggled.

"Jacob, how about you?" Mrs. Magill asked. "Can you answer my question?"

Jacob was new to the class. No one had heard him speak since he arrived.

Jacob looked down at the floor. Mrs. Magill feared she had embarrassed him. However, a moment later he looked up.

"You told us that repenting meant being sorry for the wrong things we have done. Oh, it also includes meaning never to do them again."

The young man's answer amazed Mrs. Magill.

Jacob continued, "Last week we read in the Bible about John the Baptist. He said one fruit of repenting is being honest with other people. Another is also giving away our extra clothes to someone who has none. If we have extra food, we should share it with those who are hungry."

"Great answer, Jacob," Josh Hunter said, leaning forward from the seat behind and slapping him on the back.

"Yes, it was," Mrs. Magill agreed. "Thank you, Jacob."

Jacob blushed from the attention, but he smiled.

"Does anyone have any ideas about how we might follow the Bible's instructions about helping others?" Mrs. Magill asked.

Liz Hunter's hand waved in the air.

"Yes, Liz."

"Our dad went to New York City a few weeks ago to spend some time with a friend that helps with the Raven Truck ministry."

"Raven Truck?" Sonia said. "Does it fly?"

"No, it doesn't fly," Liz answered. "It feeds people. It's like a big delivery truck with a kitchen in the back. My dad went with his friend and a few others to feed the homeless people."

"What a wonderful idea," Mrs. Magill said. "But do we have to go all the way to New York City to give food to people who are hungry?"

"No, you sure don't," Alex Webster said. "I'm starving right now. Can I have another doughnut?"

Several cheered and begged for extra doughnuts also.

"I know we all use the word *starving* to say that we're hungry," Mrs. Magill said. "But does anyone in here really know what it feels like to go without food for several days? Has anyone been outside in the cold or rain and not had a coat to put on?"

Mrs. Magill waited to see if anyone would answer her questions, then she continued.

"People need to see God's love in us. The Bible is the Truth of God that people need to hear. But they will not listen until they first see God's love through us. Now let's think of some ways we can show that love to those that are in need right here in our own city."

The class was quiet for a few moments. Mrs. Magill could see that they were really thinking about her question. Then hands began to raise.

"We can give our extra clothes," Ellen said.

"We can buy extra food each time we go to the store and give it to someone who's hungry," Mark added.

The rest of the class time focused on helping people in need. The participation pleased Mrs. Magill. She knew they should not just sit and talk about these ideas, but they should follow through with action.

CHAPTER 3

Shake, Rattle, but No Roll

Mary didn't know anything about cars, but the rattling noise from under the hood didn't sound like good news. Since leaving Dallas six hours earlier, they had stopped three times to have someone check the engine. Now all that remained of her $60 paycheck was a $10 bill.

As darkness swallowed the setting sun, lights from the next city came into view.

"Mom, we're not going to make it to Kansas with the car running like this," Blake said.

Emy was asleep in the backseat.

"No, we're not, Blake. I just don't know what to do. We don't have the money for a motel room."

The rattling from under the hood grew louder.

"We could pull off somewhere and sleep in the car," Blake suggested. "We've done that before."

Mary had been thinking the same thought. But in a strange city, where was a safe place to pull off and park?

"Where are we anyway, Mom?" Blake asked.

"Oklahoma City," Mary answered as she exited the highway. "This looks as good as any place to look for somewhere to stop," she said.

After driving a few blocks, they found themselves in a shabby neighborhood near downtown Oklahoma City.

"We don't want to park around here," she whispered to herself.

Suddenly, what had sounded like a rattle in the engine began to sound like a sledgehammer. Mary did not want to stop on the street. She pulled into the driveway of a house with boarded-up windows. She turned the engine off.

Emy continued to sleep quietly in the backseat. Blake turned to look at his mother, who sat silently staring out the window. A clap of thunder startled them, then drops of rain began to fall on the car.

"Mom, let's rest here for a while," Blake said softly. "No one will bother us when it's raining."

Mary said nothing but continued to stare out the front window. As the rain began to fall harder, so did the tears running down her cheeks.

✳ ✳ ✳

Back in Dallas, Lenny pulled himself onto the fire escape of an old apartment building. The rusted iron stairs of the escape zigzagged to the top floor five stories above. Lenny climbed the stairs to the third floor and pushed hard on the rotten outside door. After several hard shoves it opened, and he entered the third floor hallway.

The floor creaked as he walked slowly down the hall, looking at the numbers on the doors. When he came to the door marked 3-A, he stopped. Lenny looked up and down the hallway to make sure no one was around, then put his ear to the door to listen. He heard nothing. Pulling a large screwdriver from in-

side his coat, Lenny shoved it between the lock and the door and pulled back hard. The thin door gave a crunch and popped open.

Quickly, Lenny went inside and shut the door behind him. His heart sank as he looked around the room.

"They left," he said in a hoarse whisper, seeing the empty closets and bare rooms.

Lenny sank to the floor and covered his face with his hands. "I'm as good as dead!" he moaned.

✳ ✳ ✳

Mary woke up. It took her a moment to remember where she was. As soon as she tried to move, her aching muscles reminded her she had been sleeping in a car. Blake lay across most of the front seat. Mary had just enough room to scrunch up next to the door.

"What was that?" she said with a start. Something had tapped on the back window.

She looked through the rear window, seeing nothing in the darkness. Then a person's figure passed along the side of the car. Mary held her breath as she put her arm around Blake. Emy was too far away for her to reach.

Just then lightning flashed, and for a moment Mary saw a man standing a few feet from the car. Her heart beat wildly as she strained to see out the darkened windows.

CHAPTER 4

What Does Jesus Look Like?

"Ma'am, are you all right?" said a voice from outside the car. A flashlight beam shone through the darkness onto Mary's face. She raised her arm to shield her eyes.

"What do you want? Please leave us alone," Mary said, trying to think of how to protect her children.

"Don't be afraid, ma'am, I'm a police officer," the voice outside the car said. The man stood back from the car and shone the flashlight on himself.

He wore a rain jacket, and Mary could see his police officer's cap. As another flash of lightning lit the sky, Mary saw a black-and-white police car parked by the curb.

"We're having car problems," Mary said.

"Open your hood, and let me have a look," the officer said.

Mary reached under the dash and pulled the lever to unlock the hood. The police officer opened it and looked inside.

"Try to start it," he said.

Mary turned the key. A loud clanking sound came from the engine, but the car would not start. The

police officer held up his hand for her to stop, then shut the hood and walked around to Mary's window.

"I'm afraid this car's not going anywhere, ma'am," he said, wiping some grease from his hands with a handkerchief.

Mary rolled her window down a few inches.

"I'm not a mechanic, but it sounds like a rod has broken inside the engine. You'll need to tow it to a garage. Do you live around here, ma'am?"

"No. We're on our way to Wichita, Kansas," Mary said.

"May I see your driver's license, please?" the officer asked.

Mary reached for her purse and pulled out her license. The officer looked at it carefully, then returned it to Mary.

"Would you like me to call a tow truck for you, ma'am?" he asked.

Tears began to run down Mary's cheeks again, but she quickly brushed them away. "No, thank you," she said.

Then she checked the time on her watch. "It will be daylight soon. And it looks as if the rain has let up. I saw an all-night restaurant a few blocks back. We'll just walk up there and call for a tow as soon as it's light."

"I guess that will be OK," the officer said, "but move it soon. I'll come back in a couple of hours. If the car is still here, I'm afraid I'll have to have it towed."

Mary nodded that she understood but said nothing as she rolled her window up.

Blake and Emy continued to sleep soundly. Mary would wait until it was light to wake them.

                    ✱ ✱ ✱

They drank coffee and hot chocolate. Mary, Blake, and Emy warmed up at a corner table as a plate of biscuits quickly disappeared in front of them. Blake reached hungrily for his third one. After paying for breakfast, Mary figured they would have less than $6 left.

"Mom, what are we going to do about the car?" Blake asked between bites.

Mary didn't answer. She just stared into her coffee mug. She didn't have any idea what to do.

"Let's call Grandma in Wichita," Emy said. "She'll come and help us."

"No!" Mary said sharply, a little louder than she had meant to. "I don't even know if your grandmother wants to see us."

Emy was just a baby the last time she had seen her grandmother, but Blake had told her stories about how nice she was.

"I'm sorry, Emy. I didn't mean to snap at you," Mary said.

The man sitting at the table next to the Redmans had been watching the young mother and her two children since they sat down. From what he overheard, he could tell they were having troubles.

The man smiled. Just this morning he had prayed, "Lord, please send me to someone who needs to know Your love, and let me show it to them."

Clearing his throat, he caught the young mother's attention. "Excuse me," he said, "could I be of any help to you?"

CHAPTER 5

Old Henry

"AAAAAAA!"

"It just ran under the bookcase!"

"No, it's heading for that pile of clothes!"

Josh and Liz Hunter each held a broom. They crept between rows of hanging shirts, pants, and dresses in the Love-Link Ministries warehouse. They were on fall break from school and were helping their mother sort donated clothing for people who needed assistance.

"Look out, Liz, it's heading right for you," Josh said to his sister a few rows over.

"AAAAA!" Liz screamed as she dropped her broom handle.

Josh doubled over laughing. "Got you!" he said.

As he straightened up, he glanced at the shelf that hung at eye level on his left. There, perched inches from his nose, was the biggest, hairiest, ugliest rat he had ever seen.

"AAAAAAAA!" Josh screamed as he ran to jump up on a nearby table. Liz was close behind.

The rat jumped off the shelf and scurried out a hole the size of a quarter in the warehouse wall.

This time it was Liz who doubled over with laughter.

"Well, great hunter, it's nice to have you here protecting me," Liz giggled.

"Did you see the size of that thing? That wasn't a rat; it was some kind of mutant dog," Josh said.

Mrs. Hunter had been in the kitchen helping prepare the Thursday lunch. She walked in to find her 9- and 10-year-old children standing on the shoe table.

"Get down from there. What in the world are you two doing?" she asked.

"Mom, the King Kong of rats attacked us," Josh exclaimed.

"Rats?" Mrs. Hunter said, stopping suddenly.

"That's right, Mom. It almost kissed Josh on the nose," Liz said, still giggling.

Josh and Liz climbed down from the table and walked back to the box of clothes they had been sorting. Mrs. Hunter joined them, looking around the room cautiously as she walked. As an emergency room nurse, she was a tough woman. But she couldn't handle rats or mice.

Walter, another volunteer worker, walked in from the other room after hearing talk of rats.

"You must have met Old Henry," he said, stroking his thick gray beard.

"Henry? You mean the rat has a name?" Liz asked.

"He sure enough does," Walter said. "Named him myself, after my cousin Henry. Cousin Henry liked to take items that weren't his, just like that old rat does. Spent some time in jail for it too."

"The rat's been in jail?" Liz asked.

"No, my cousin. Course, I can't say about the rat one way or another."

"The rat takes things?" Josh asked. "What kinds of things?"

"Oh, he'll take gum wrappers, shoes, anything lying around." Walter could tell that Mrs. Hunter didn't like the thought of a rat big enough to carry off a shoe. With a twinkle in his eye he added, "It would have gotten away with that frozen turkey a few weeks ago. But he couldn't get it through the hole in the wall."

Mrs. Hunter and Liz both gasped in horror at the thought. Josh stared wide-eyed at the hole Henry had escaped through. Then Mrs. Hunter caught the big grin on Walter's face. She laughed and tossed an old shirt at him.

"Oh, you're a big teaser, Walter," she said.

Walter turned around and went back into the large dining hall, laughing all the way.

The Hunters went back to their work sorting the donated clothing.

"Mom, who gives these clothes to Love-Link?" Liz asked.

"People bring clothes they don't wear anymore to places like Love-Link so others who need them can use them."

"I understand about giving away clothes that you don't wear anymore," Liz said, "but some of these look more like rags than used clothing."

"Yeah, check out these pants," Josh said. He held them up and put his hand through a giant hole in the seat.

"People sometimes forget who they are really giving to," Mrs. Hunter said.

"What do you mean?" Josh asked.

"Remember Jesus' words in Matthew 25, 'I tell you the truth, whatever you did for one of the least of these brothers of mine, you did for me' (v. 40). When we give something to people who are needy, we are giving to Jesus," Mrs. Hunter said.

"I wonder, would someone have given those pants if they thought they were a gift to Jesus?" Liz asked.

"I hope not," Mrs. Hunter replied. She reached into the bottom of the box and pulled out the last item, a pair of old brown pants. It looked as if a dog had chewed the legs off.

CHAPTER 6

More than Words

Delightful smells floated from the kitchen into the clothing room where the Hunters worked. Each Thursday at 11:30, people at Love-Link Ministries served lunch to anyone off the street who was hungry. There were lots of different people who came. Some were homeless. Others lived in government housing projects. But they all had one thing in common. They all needed to hear that Jesus loved them. They felt that love through the hands of the ministry volunteers.

Josh and Liz raced into the dining hall while their mother walked behind them. Soon the three noticed Walter talking with a young woman. A little girl hung to the woman's arm, while a boy, probably about Josh's age, stood next to her. When Walter saw the Hunters, he waved for them to come over.

"Mary Redman, I would like you to meet Rusti Hunter and her two children, Josh and Liz," Walter said. "These are Mary's children, Blake and Emy."

After shaking hands, Walter explained that he had met Mary and the children that morning at a restaurant. "These folks are on their way to Wichita, Kansas, but they're having some serious car trouble," Walter said.

"Oh, no," Mrs. Hunter said. "Where is your car now?"

Mary smiled at Walter and explained, "This kind man called a friend. He came and towed it back to his auto repair shop. He will let me know what is wrong this afternoon."

Walter acted a bit embarrassed by Mary's reference to him.

Then he remembered something. "Rusti, I almost forgot. Here are your car keys." He fumbled in his pants pocket and pulled out a set of keys. "It took a couple of us to load it, but we put Mrs. Leever's kitchen sink in the back of your van. Make sure your husband doesn't try to unload it tomorrow morning before I get there."

"Thanks, Walter, I'll tell him," Mrs. Hunter promised.

Josh laughed. "How many sinks will this make for Mrs. Leever?" he asked.

Mrs. Hunter turned to Mary to explain. "Mrs. Leever is an elderly woman."

"A very cranky elderly woman," Liz interrupted.

Mrs. Hunter smiled. "Her back hurts her a lot, so she's not always in a good mood. We need to replace her kitchen sink. But every time we arrange to get one for her, something happens to it."

"It's kind of become a joke around here," Josh said.

"Not to Mrs. Leever," Liz giggled. "She tried to hit Dad with her cane when he told her about the last one. It bounced off the truck into the river."

"Well, you folks find a place to sit," Walter finally said. "We'll have a short devotion, then we'll eat."

People quickly began to fill the dining area. Some came by themselves, but most came in groups of two or three. It was safer on the street if you stayed close to someone else. Some carried sacks or bags that contained all of their possessions. Others wandered in, wearing everything they owned.

Mary, Blake, and Emy found a seat at one of the tables. Liz decided there was plenty of help in the kitchen, so she sat down next to Emy.

"Do you have friends in Wichita?" Liz asked Mary.

Emy answered for her. "My grandma lives in Wichita! We're going to go see her."

Mary started to correct her daughter by saying she wasn't sure what they would be doing in Wichita. But a man stepped to the front of the room and began speaking before she had a chance.

The man opened a Bible and began reading the words of Jesus.

"Come to Me, all who are weary and heavy-laden, and I will give you rest. Take My yoke upon you, and learn from Me, for I am gentle and humble in heart; and you shall find rest for your souls" (Matthew 11:28-29, NASB).

As he read the words, Mary felt a strange sensation. It was as if someone had placed a heating pad on her heart. She had felt this way this morning, too, when Walter helped with her car.

"Maybe I'm finally moving in the right direction," she whispered to herself.

After the devotional time was over, several volunteers began to carry plates of food to the tables.

"Sussgetty, my favorite!" Emy said with excitement as a man placed a plate of steaming spaghetti and meat sauce in front of her.

After everyone received food, Mrs. Hunter and Josh grabbed plates and sat down to eat with Mary, Blake, Emy, and Liz.

"Can we give you a ride over to the repair shop, Mary?" Mrs. Hunter asked.

"That would be very nice, but we don't want to put you to any trouble," Mary responded.

"No trouble at all," Liz and Josh said at the same time.

"Do you think I could make a telephone call back to Dallas?" Mary asked. "The woman that lived in the apartment next to ours is checking our mailbox. The company that laid me off is sending me a check for the sick pay they owe me. My boss said it would be a day or two before they mailed it. It won't be much, but it might help get the car repaired."

"We can work that out," Mrs. Hunter said, smiling. "Josh, you and Liz keep Blake and Emy company while I show Mary where the phone is."

"I have a few dollars to cover the phone charge," Mary said, digging into the pocket of her jeans.

"No, no, that won't be necessary," Mrs. Hunter said. "This call is on us."

As she showed Mary to the office, Mrs. Hunter saw all four children scurry back into the clothing room. She heard Josh saying to Blake, "We want to introduce you to our friend, Old Henry."

CHAPTER 7

The Chase Begins

Mrs. Peterson's shoes made a swishing sound as her fluffy slippers shuffled across the old carpet of her small living room.

Ringggg. Ringggg.

"I'm coming, I'm coming," she said as she moved toward the telephone. "This is as fast as these old legs will take me."

"Hello," she said.

"Well hello, Mary. How are you and the children?"

Mrs. Peterson listened as Mary explained her situation.

"I'm so sorry, dear. Is there anything I can do?"

Mary gave Mrs. Peterson the phone number of Love-Link Ministries. She told her they would know how to reach her during the next day or so.

"So you want me to call when the check comes and find out where to send it, is that right? OK, Mary, I'll be happy to. Give Blake and Emy a big hug for me. Oh, my arthritis? Yes, it's hurting in this cool weather, but I'll be fine. Thank you for asking, though. Good-bye."

As Mrs. Peterson hung up the phone, there was a knock at her door. She walked stiffly to the peephole to see who was there. A scruffy-looking young man stood looking back at her. She didn't recognize him.

"Can I help you?" she said without opening the door.

"I'm sorry to bother you, ma'am," the young man said. "I was wondering if you knew where my sister is."

"Your sister? I don't even know who you are. How would I know where your sister is? What's your name?"

"Lenny, ma'am. My sister lived next door."

❋ ❋ ❋

"The repair shop is on the next block, Mrs. Hunter," Mary said from the passenger side of the Hunters' van.

"Yes, I see it, and please call me Rusti."

As they drove up, Mrs. Hunter turned to talk to the children in the back. "You four wait here while Mary and I go talk with the service person."

Mrs. Hunter followed Mary into the old metal garage. At first they didn't see anyone. Then Mary noticed a pair of legs sticking out from under a blue pickup truck.

"Hello," Mary said suddenly to the pair of feet sticking out.

A voice from under the truck let out a yelp. Then the legs came scooting out from under the truck. It was Walter's friend, Jack Harding. As he rolled out, he was holding his head.

"You scared me," Jack said.

"I'm sorry," Mary said. "I just stopped by to see what you found out about my car."

Jack Harding stood and wiped his hands on the legs of his coveralls. "Well, ma'am, it doesn't look too good, I'm afraid," Jack said as he walked over to a cluttered desk. He picked up a clipboard with a paper attached. He scanned the paper as he talked.

"The engine is in pretty bad shape. Walter told me about your situation. There won't be any charge for labor to fix your car. But the parts will cost close to $350."

"Three hundred and fifty dollars!" Mary said, her face turning pale. "I need to find a job real fast," she said weakly.

She sat down on an old wooden bench next to the desk, her mind racing. Where could she stay? Where could she find work? How would she get to work without a car?

"Will the problems ever stop?" she finally said.

Mrs. Hunter sat down next to her and put her arm around Mary's shoulders. "I can't say when the problems are going to stop, Mary. But I can tell you that you won't have to face them alone."

Mary looked up at Mrs. Hunter. Alone was exactly how she had felt for a long time. People had disappointed her so many times that she had stopped trusting anyone. She thought it might be different this time because of Walter's kindness that morning. The words read from the Bible and now Mrs. Hunter sitting next to her gave her hope.

"Let's go back to the Love-Link office and see what we can figure out," Mrs. Hunter said. "Mr. Harding, will you keep Mary's car here until she decides what to do?"

"Of course; just let me know in a couple of days."

Mary pulled a tissue from her pocket and wiped tears away from her eyes. "I'll need to get the rest of our bags out of the car," she said.

"I'll help you," Mrs. Hunter offered.

Jack went back to work on the pickup truck. Mary and Mrs. Hunter walked out to the old station wagon. Mary grabbed two duffel bags from the back of the car while Mrs. Hunter grabbed a backpack sitting on the backseat.

"Oh, what's this?" Mrs. Hunter said to herself. She reached for a red strap sticking out from under the front seat. She pulled it out. It was another backpack.

"I almost missed this," she said to Mary, holding up the red pack.

Mary looked at the pack. "I don't recognize it," she said. "It must be something Emy found."

They loaded the bags into the van and drove back to the Love-Link office.

❊　❊　❊

"Hello, this is Love-Link Ministries; can I help you?" the secretary said as she answered the phone.

A raspy voice at the other end of the line demanded, "Give me directions to your office."

"I'll be happy to, sir. Where will you be coming from?"

"Dallas," was all the voice said.

CHAPTER 8

Love in Action

"How much is it, Mom?" Blake asked doubtfully. He was always the practical one in the family.

He and Mary stood in the front room of a small furnished house two miles from the Love-Link warehouse. Mary turned to Walter and Mrs. Hunter with the same question.

Walter smiled. "My wife and I call this the Hospitality House. We keep it for people who need a place to stay for a short time. There's no charge. We just ask that you keep it clean for the next people who need to use it."

"You mean we can stay here for free?" Mary asked in disbelief.

Walter nodded his head yes.

"We're perfect strangers, yet you've helped us with our car, you've fed us, and now you're giving us a place to stay. Who are you people?" Mary asked.

"Just people who love Jesus, you, and your children," Mrs. Hunter answered. "We want you to know how much Jesus loves you too."

Mary stood staring at Walter and Mrs. Hunter. Then she turned to look out the window. It was several moments before she spoke.

"We've been having a hard time for the last five years. I find work for a while, but then something always happens, and I lose my job. Church people have helped us from time to time. But none of them cared what happened to us after they gave us food or clothes. I guess part of that was my fault. I never gave anyone the chance to get close to us. But you've been different. You care about us. For the first time in many years I'm actually starting to think that maybe God doesn't hate me."

"God doesn't hate you, Mary. He loves you," Mrs. Hunter said. "He has always loved you. He stretches out His arms, waiting for you to come to Him."

Before Mary could respond, Emy came running in the house. She carried the red backpack Mrs. Hunter had removed from the back of the station wagon. Liz and Josh were right behind her.

"Mommy! Mommy! We can fix the car now," Emy said excitedly.

She shoved the backpack into Mary's hands. Mary looked inside and couldn't believe what she was seeing.

There, in the backpack, was money. Lots of money.

* * *

In Viper Grimes's apartment, Lenny sat on the edge of an old sofa. A black metal spring poked through the fabric next to his leg. Lenny shifted nervously as he listened to Viper talk on the phone. He wanted to be anywhere but in Viper's apartment.

Viper slammed down the receiver and walked over to Lenny. "Tell me one more time what the old lady said," Viper hissed.

Lenny cleared his throat, trying to keep his voice steady.

"She was talking on the phone to the lady with the two kids just before I knocked on her door. I told her I was looking for my sister, and she believed me." Lenny looked up at Viper, hoping to impress him with how he had fooled the elderly woman.

Viper just glared at him and snarled, "Tell me what she said."

"She said that Mary—that's the lady's name that drives the old station wagon—left for Kansas, but her car broke down in Oklahoma City. She gave me the number you just called. I guess the people there are helping her out. She gave me an address too."

Viper snatched the paper with the address from Lenny's hand.

"Let's go," Viper said.

"Wha . . . wha . . . what do you mean, *let's* go?" Lenny stammered. "You don't want *me* to go along?"

Viper grabbed Lenny by the collar and yanked him to his feet. "That's exactly what I want, Weasel," Viper said. "If it turns out you've been lying to me, you'll be staying in Oklahoma permanently."

Viper shoved Lenny toward the door, then checked his watch. "It's 1:15 now. We should be in Oklahoma City by 4:30 this afternoon. That should give us enough time to track down this lady and her two brats before dark." Then his lips twisted into an evil grin. "We'll wait until dark to go after her, though. I work best in the dark."

CHAPTER 9

They Know Who I Am

"Look, Mommy, we've got all the money we need!" Emy exclaimed excitedly.

Mary continued to stare wide-eyed at the bundles of $20 bills inside the backpack.

"Where did you find this?" Mary finally asked.

"It was with the stuff you pulled out of our car," Emy answered.

Mrs. Hunter looked at Mary. "Remember, that's the pack I asked you about. It was under the seat of your car."

Mary remembered. She slowly sat down on one of the living room chairs, the color draining from her face.

Emy saw the look. "Mommy, what's the matter? God gave us the money so we won't be poor anymore. You should be happy." She walked over and patted her mother's hand.

"I have a pretty good idea who gave us the money, Emy, and it wasn't God," Mary said.

"We lived in a rough part of Dallas," Mary continued, looking up at Walter and Mrs. Hunter. "The drug dealers don't even try to hide what they are doing. That's where I think the money came from. The locks don't work on our car. Someone must have used it to hide money from a drug deal."

"Drug money—wow!" Josh said. He and Liz had been standing by the front door. "Do you think the dealers know where it is?" he asked.

"If it's who I think it is, he'll find out pretty fast. After hiding the money, I'm sure he expected to come right back and get it. We must have driven away before he had a chance," Mary said.

She covered her face with her hands. "Oh no," she said. "The only way someone would take a chance on hiding that much money in a car is if the person knew who drove it."

"I don't understand, Mom," Blake said. "It doesn't matter if he knows our car; we're more than 200 miles away from there now."

"I agree," said Walter. "There's not much a drug dealer from Dallas can do in Oklahoma City. We should contact the police and let them handle it."

Mary continued to look pale and frightened. She looked down at the money again and shook her head. "You don't know these people. They'll shoot you if you look at them the wrong way. They won't stop searching for me if they think I have their money."

"But they can't know who you are, Mary," Mrs. Hunter said.

"Dallas is like other big cities," Mary answered. "Gangs handle most of the drug dealing. Gang members have to know who lives on their block. They also have to know what cars the people drive. That way they recognize the outsiders."

"But there's no way they could know where you are now, Mary," Mrs. Hunter said.

Mary's face looked even paler. "That might have been true before I called Mrs. Peterson, the woman that lived next door to us. I told her where we are."

* * *

Lenny stood at a gas station 30 miles south of Oklahoma City. He placed his hand over one ear and pressed the telephone receiver hard against his other ear. It was still too noisy to hear well.

"Is it ringing?" Viper yelled from the window of his black pickup truck parked in front of the pay phone.

Lenny nodded his head.

"Hello, this is Love-Link Ministries," the secretary said from the other end of the line.

"Hello," Lenny said. "Is Mary Redman there?"

"I'm sorry. I don't believe I know that name," the secretary said.

"She and her two kids had some car trouble and left me this number. My name's Lenny. I'm her brother." Lenny shifted his weight from foot to foot as he always did when he lied.

"Oh yes, I know who you mean," the woman said. "She's not here, but I know where she is staying."

"Can you give me the address? I've got some money for her to get the car fixed," Lenny said.

"Of course, how nice of you. Let me give you the directions too."

Lenny tore out a page from a phone book attached to the wall and wrote down the information.

"If I see her, what time should I tell her you'll be here?" the woman asked.

"Don't tell her anything," Lenny answered excitedly. Then, not wanting the woman to become suspicious, he explained, "Sis never thinks I'm around to help when she needs me. I want to surprise her.

Thanks for your help." Then Lenny hung up the phone and went back to the car.

Viper snatched the torn page from Lenny's hand and looked at the address and directions. "It looks as if you were telling me the truth, Weasel," he sneered.

Then he looked at his watch. "We'll take care of this problem and be back in Dallas by midnight."

"Viper, the lady and her kids probably don't know anything about the money in their car. We just want the money back, right?" Lenny asked nervously.

Viper just laughed as he drove the car out of the gas station and back onto the highway.

CHAPTER 10

A Prayer for Help

Dr. Hunter pulled up to the Love-Link Ministries warehouse. He noticed Walter's car and his wife's van parked next to the building. A police car was also there. When his wife had called, asking if he could drop by the Love-Link office, she said there was a small problem. If the police were here, he guessed it was more than a small problem.

"Dad!" Josh and Liz said together as Dr. Hunter walked through the front door. They ran up and both began explaining the Redmans' situation.

"They're going to Kansas . . . their car broke down . . . they slept in their car . . . lots of money . . . it was drug money . . . gangs are after them . . ."

"Hold on a minute," Dr. Hunter said, putting up his hands. "With both of you talking, I can't understand anything you're saying."

Just then Mrs. Hunter walked out of the office. "Hi, sweetheart," she said. "I'm so glad you're here."

"What's going on, Rusti? I saw a police car outside, and the kids said something about drug money," Dr. Hunter said.

"Come on in the office; I want you to meet someone. Then we'll tell you what we know."

As Mrs. Hunter led her husband into the office, Blake and Emy appeared from the back of the warehouse. They walked up to Josh and Liz.

"I found her," Blake said. He had his arm around his sister. Emy was still sniffling from crying.

After hearing her mother talk about the money, Emy had become very frightened. She didn't want a gang to find them. When they arrived at the Love-Link office to call the police, Emy had run into the warehouse to hide.

Liz sat down on a bench and pulled Emy onto her lap. Even at five years, Emy was very small.

"Don't cry, Emy," she said, stroking the little girl's hair.

"But bad people are coming after us, and it's my fault," Emy whimpered.

"We don't know if any bad people are after you or not. And it is not your fault," Liz assured her. "My dad's here now, and so are the police. Everything will be fine."

"Having the police around doesn't mean we're safe. And it doesn't mean everything will be fine," Blake said sadly.

"But there's someone else here too," Josh said. "He can keep us safe even if no one else can."

"Who?" Emy asked, sitting up straight on Liz's lap and looking around.

"Jesus, that's who," Liz answered.

"My grandmother used to tell me about God when I was little," Blake said. "But we haven't heard much about Him in a long time. So what does He do—send angels out to protect us?"

"Something like that," Josh answered, smiling at Liz. "Last year in Brazil God protected our family from evil people. Just take our word for it—the best thing we can do right now is pray."

Emy immediately put her hands together and shut her eyes. "Now I lay me down to sleep," she began.

"No, Emy, that's for bedtime," Blake said kindly.

Emy looked up. "That's the only prayer I know."

"We really don't know much about praying," Blake said. "Maybe you could show us, Josh."

"Sure." Then Josh closed his eyes and began to pray.

"Lord, I know You already know what's been going on, and I thank You for watching over us. We all need Your protection. Help Emy not to be afraid anymore. If there is something bad about that money, please show Mrs. Redman what to do. Amen."

✳   ✳   ✳

"As I said, Mrs. Redman, we'll take the pack and the money to police headquarters. I will lock it up," Officer Wilson of the Oklahoma City police department said. "We'll call the Dallas police and see if there is a report of missing money. My guess is that it's money from a drug deal, just as you suspect."

"What happens to the money in that case?" Dr. Hunter asked.

"Since Mrs. Redman found it, if no one claims it in 60 days, she gets to keep it. If we find the dealer, we'll keep it as evidence and use it to convict the person."

Mary shuddered. "I don't want anything to do with that money. I want to get my car fixed and get as far away from here as I can."

"Mrs. Redman, please don't worry," Officer Wilson said. "We'll alert the officer patrolling this area to pay close attention to the house where you'll be staying. Here's my beeper number. Please call if anything else comes up." He then turned and left, carrying the red backpack filled with the money.

"Mrs. Hunter, will you please take us back to the house now? It's getting dark outside. I want to feed the kids and get them to bed early."

"Certainly. We need to be getting home ourselves," Mrs. Hunter answered. They walked out of the office and called for the children.

"Do you want to meet us at home, sweetheart?" she asked her husband as she headed for the front door.

"No. I want to talk with Walter for a moment longer, then I'll catch up with you."

The phone rang, and Walter picked it up.

"Hello, Love-Link Ministries." Walter listened. "She just left. . . . He said what? . . . When was this? . . . OK, thank you for calling."

Walter hung up the phone and gave Dr. Hunter a worried look.

"That was Lucy Widel. She was helping answer the phones in the office this afternoon. She had a funny feeling about one of the calls she got just before she left. She thought she should let someone know about it."

"Who was the call from?" Dr. Hunter asked.

"From a man saying he was Mary Redman's brother. He asked for directions to where they're staying and said he had some money for her."

"Did Lucy give him the information?"

"Yes. She said he was polite at first. Then Lucy said he got upset when she asked what time she should tell Mary he would arrive. He said it was to be a surprise."

"Walter, I heard Mary tell the police officer that her only family was her children and her mother in Kansas."

Suddenly, both men realized Mary was in danger. They turned and raced to Dr. Hunter's car. Each prayed they could catch up to the van in time.

CHAPTER 11

Trapped

Clang, clang, clang, clang.

"Mom, we just missed counting the cars on the 6:00 train," Liz said disappointedly. She looked out the back window of the van. Red lights flashed as the crossbars dropped over the railroad tracks behind them.

"I'm glad we missed it tonight, dear," Mrs. Hunter said. "The 6:00 train can be a hundred cars long, and we need to get Mary and the children to the hospitality house."

Mrs. Hunter turned the van onto Southwest 38th and drove four blocks down the dark street before arriving in front of the small hospitality house.

The only other car on the dark street was a black pickup truck parked by the curb two blocks back.

* * *

"Oh no, we're cut off by the train," Walter said.

Dr. Hunter stopped at the crossbars, pounding his hand against the steering wheel in frustration. The red flashing lights reflected on the men's faces.

"Can we turn around and go down another street?" Dr. Hunter asked.

"No. The train blocks all the streets along here. The fastest way is to wait for it to pass," Walter said.

Dr. Hunter picked up his car phone and tried for the fourth time to reach his wife. "She always forgets to turn her phone on," he said.

Suddenly the train lurched and, with a loud screech, began to slow down.

"What's happening, Walter?"

"It looks as if they're attaching another car. They'll come to a stop, then back up to connect the new car."

"This is an emergency; they've got to let us through first." Dr. Hunter started to get out of the car, but Walter put his hand on his shoulder.

"Doc, there's nothing you or that train engineer can do to speed up this train. All we can do is wait and pray."

Dr. Hunter closed his car door. "OK, Walter, let's start praying."

* * *

Mary and Mrs. Hunter walked up the driveway leading to the front door. Mary asked if she would go in with her to check out the house before the children came in.

"I know it sounds silly," she said. "Both of us could go in and turn on all the lights and check under the beds and in the closets. The kids and I would feel a lot better."

Before reaching the house, Mrs. Hunter turned to Mary and said, "We have an extra room. Why don't you and the children stay with us tonight?"

"Thank you, Mrs. Hunter—I mean Rusti. But we couldn't do that."

"Please, Mary. It wouldn't be any trouble, and I know you and the children are nervous about staying here tonight. Besides, the children are all getting along so well."

"Why are they just standing there talking?" Josh said, looking out the van window at his mother and Mary.

"Who knows?" Blake answered. "They are probably trying to decide—"

Liz's excited voice from the back of the van interrupted Blake. "There it goes again! I told you it was moving!"

Liz and Emy were sitting in the far backseat of the van, looking out the rear window. Now Josh and Blake turned to look.

"That black truck has been moving up the street with its lights off," Liz whispered. "We passed it several blocks back, but now look at it."

Josh and Blake leaned over their seats for a better look.

"I see the truck, Liz, but why would it be moving without its lights on? That's crazy!" Josh said.

Then he froze. The truck was moving, and it looked as if it was picking up speed.

Suddenly the truck's headlights flashed on. Its tires screeched as it swerved for the driveway of the hospitality house, heading directly for Mary and Mrs. Hunter.

✳ ✳ ✳

Clang, clang, clang, clang.

"Come on, come on," Dr. Hunter said as the last two cars of the train went by.

As soon as it passed, Dr. Hunter raced through, almost hitting the crossbars as they lifted.

"Which street do we turn on, Walter? I've forgotten."

"38th Street," Walter replied.

Dr. Hunter calculated the distance in his head. "We're still a mile away," he muttered, as he pressed his foot harder on the gas.

CHAPTER 12

A Sink to the Rescue

Mary froze as she stared at the glaring headlights of the black truck speeding toward her. Providentially, Mrs. Hunter jumped quickly into action.

"Run, Mary!" she said, grabbing Mary's arm and sprinting toward the van.

The truck turned into the driveway, hitting a trash can and spewing garbage everywhere. The can flew into the air and smashed against the truck's windshield. It didn't damage the truck. The truck slowed down for an instant, which gave Mrs. Hunter and Mary time to reach the van and jump inside.

Mrs. Hunter fumbled for the keys as the truck screeched to a halt just a few feet away. "O God, deliver us from this evil," she prayed.

"Hurry, Mom, they're getting out of the truck!" Liz yelled.

Suddenly, something crashed against the passenger side door.

Mrs. Hunter looked up to see a man's face and hands pressed up against the window. A baseball bat was in his right hand.

Finally, she found the key and started the engine. The man outside began to slam the bat into the window as Mrs. Hunter stomped her foot on the gas pedal and raced away. The bat missed the window and struck the side door.

"Mary, grab my purse and get my cellular phone."

Mary opened Mrs. Hunter's purse and tried to find the cellular phone in the darkness.

Mrs. Hunter looked in the rearview mirror and saw that the black truck was now following and gaining fast.

"OK, I found it," Mary said.

"Push the power button to turn it on, then call 911."

"He's going to hit us from behind!" Josh screamed from the back.

"All of you get your heads down!" Mrs. Hunter yelled back over her shoulder. The four children all scrunched down in their seats.

At the next intersection she turned left, went a block, then turned left again. Checking her rearview mirror again, she saw that the truck was not as close. But it was still following them.

"They want to know what street we're on," Mary said, holding the phone to her ear.

Mrs. Hunter made another sharp left. "Tell them we're heading south on Western Avenue toward 44th Street."

Thump! The van lurched forward as the truck bumped them from behind.

Josh suddenly poked his head up. "Mom, I've got an idea!"

Mrs. Hunter was too busy driving to hear him.

Josh crawled to the backseat where Liz and Emy huddled. He then leaned over them to unlock the back door.

"What are you doing, Josh?" Liz asked. "Mom said to keep our heads down!"

Ignoring his sister, Josh pried off a small panel on the door, revealing a metal lever about two inches long.

"Josh, you're crazy! Sit down before you get hurt," Liz said. "Besides, you can't open the door while we're moving."

"Want to bet?" Josh said. He grabbed the lever and pulled hard to his left. There was the sound of a click at the bottom of the door. Josh pushed gently, and it began to raise. He grabbed the handle to hold it closed for a moment.

The truck had pulled back a short distance after hitting the van. Josh could see through the window that it was moving closer again.

"Look, Liz," Josh said, pointing at Mrs. Leever's kitchen sink.

Liz's eyes brightened as she understood her brother's idea. She nodded her head in agreement.

"Where are the police?" Mrs. Hunter said from the front seat.

"The 911 operator said to keep driving straight and not to turn off this street," Mary answered.

Mrs. Hunter looked in her side mirror. "Oh no, he's going to bump us again. Everybody hold on."

"Now!" Josh said, releasing his hold on the door. It popped open quickly. Liz and Josh then pushed hard on the large iron sink propped up in the back of the van. It fell over and then bounced out the open door onto the street with a loud crash.

Viper Grimes, driving the black pickup, was curious about the van's back hatch opening. A flashing red light caught his eye for a fraction of a second.

"Look out, Viper!" Lenny yelled.

Viper looked up in time to see a kitchen sink bounce on the street in front of him. He slammed his foot on the brake and tried to swerve out of the way. He was too late.

The truck was high enough that the sink passed under the grill. It crashed into the front, then the rear axles that held the wheels together. It ripped both sets of wheels out from under the truck. Viper and Lenny looked at each other helplessly. The truck body was now without wheels and still traveling at 50 miles an hour. It dropped to the ground and skidded along the asphalt.

Mrs. Hunter screamed as she heard the crash. She looked in her mirror and saw the back door was open. At first she feared that one of the children had fallen out. She quickly counted. All four were there, and they were cheering.

"Look, Rusti," Mary said, pointing behind them.

Mrs. Hunter checked again in her side mirror and saw the spinning truck. She slowed down and pulled to the side of the street. Suddenly, flashing red lights and sirens came from several directions.

A car pulled up behind them, and two men jumped out.

"It's Dad and Walter!" Liz yelled.

Rusti bowed her head and prayed, "Thank You, Father." Then she jumped out of the van and into the arms of her husband.

CHAPTER 13

Hope Renewed

It took several hours to fill out all the paperwork and answer the police officers' questions. Josh and Liz's parents scolded them for pushing Mrs. Leever's sink out of the van. Now, newspaper reporters at the scene declared them heroes.

Viper and Lenny went to jail in handcuffs.

Officer Wilson, one of the first policemen to arrive, took charge of the investigation. "Mrs. Hunter and Ms. Redman, I will need you to come down to our station tomorrow and sign the reports," he said. He made some final notes in a black notebook.

"What time should we be there?" Mrs. Hunter asked.

"The reports should be ready around 10 A.M.," Officer Wilson said. "I've already been in touch with the Dallas police department," he continued. "They connected me with the person working with the gangs in your area of town, Ms. Redman. I gave him the description of the man driving the truck. He knew exactly who I was talking about. His name is Viper Grimes. He's out of jail on parole, so this stunt of his will send him back behind bars for several years. You won't have to worry about him anymore."

"There were two men in the truck, though," Mary said.

Officer Wilson smiled. "You don't need to worry about the other one either. If his story is true, Viper forced him to come along. He's scared. If we let him, I think he'd run all the way back to Dallas and hide in a hole somewhere," he chuckled.

Mary didn't laugh. "I know what it's like to be afraid," she said.

Officer Wilson cleared his throat and looked back at his notebook. "Well, I guess that's all for tonight. I'll see you both tomorrow."

"Thank you, Officer Wilson," Mrs. Hunter said. Then, turning to Mary and using her no-nonsense voice, she said, "No arguments—you and your children are staying with us tonight. We'll talk about other arrangements in the morning."

* * *

"Would you like some more tea, Mary?" Mrs. Hunter asked.

"Yes. Thank you," Mary said, holding up her empty cup.

After cleaning up, everyone gathered around the fireplace in the Hunters' home. Emy lay with her head in Mary's lap, sleeping peacefully.

Mary sat quietly staring into the fire as she sipped her tea. No one spoke for some time. Finally, Mary set her cup down and looked up at the Hunter family.

"Do you bring every poor family you meet home to stay with you?" she asked.

"Not every one," Dr. Hunter replied, smiling.

"I didn't realize how long I'd been living without any hope in my life," Mary said. "I didn't have any joy either. A person can live without joy for a while if they have the hope that things will get better. I didn't realize how hopeless I was until I woke up this morning."

"Do you still feel hopeless, Mary?" Mrs. Hunter asked.

Mary smiled. "Hope began to come back the minute Walter stopped by our table that morning and asked if he could help. From that moment on I've been seeing . . ." Mary stopped for a moment, not sure how to put what she was feeling into words.

"This may sound funny, but the only way for me to describe it is I've been seeing Jesus all day today in all of you. I used to know what He was like when I was a young girl. I'd forgotten. I've made so many mistakes in my life, I thought God had given up on me. But now I know He hasn't. I have hope now."

"Does that include hope that you and your mother can start over?" Mrs. Hunter asked.

"I would like to start over; I'm just afraid that she might not want to talk with me. I said some pretty awful words to her before I left five years ago."

"Mary, could you ever stop loving Blake or Emy, or wanting the best for them?" Mrs. Hunter asked.

"No. Of course not," Mary answered.

"Then don't you think your mother loves and cares for you in the same way?"

Mary sat thinking for some time. Then she looked up and said, "Do you really think she wants to hear from me?"

Mrs. Hunter stood and offered her hand to help Mary up. "Come on, I'll show you where the phone is."

EPILOGUE

The old station wagon backed out of the Hunters' driveway and headed down the street. All four of the Hunters stood in the front yard, waving good-bye to Mary, Blake, and Emy.

Mary's mother had insisted that she and the children come to Wichita as soon as they could.

It had taken three days to complete the car repairs. During that time, Mary stayed with the Hunters. Each morning, Mrs. Hunter would drive Mary to the Love-Link warehouse. She put in a full day of work. The ministry paid for her car repairs in return for her working at the warehouse.

Officer Wilson had called the night before. He told them that Viper Grimes and Lenny were back in Dallas. Viper would be going to the Texas state prison. It wasn't known what would happen to Lenny. "One thing is certain," Officer Wilson said, "none of you will need to worry about them bothering you."

"Dad, when I think about other people like the Redmans, it makes me want to go do something to help them," Liz said. She watched the station wagon disappear around the corner. "But then I start thinking that I'm just a kid. There are so many people who need help, I get discouraged."

Dr. Hunter put his arm around his daughter. "Liz, I'm very glad you have the desire to help those who are in need. As followers of Jesus, that should be one of our greatest pleasures. Being young doesn't mean God can't use you to help others. Just remember

63

Jesus' method of helping people. He did it one person at a time."

"What do you mean, one person at a time?" Josh asked.

"Don't get discouraged by thinking about all the needs people have and how you could never help everyone," Dr. Hunter said. "Simply allow God to use you to make a difference in one person's life at a time."

Josh and Liz thought about what their father had said. "So who do you think we can help next?" Liz asked.

Josh started laughing. "How about Mrs. Leever?" he asked. "I think she's still waiting for her kitchen sink."